DO NOT REMOVE
CARDS FROM POCKET

10/93

For Hogan and James

Copyright © 1993 by Ken Brown
Four Winds Press Macmillan Publishing Company 866 Third Avenue New York, NY 10022
Maxwell Macmillan Canada, Inc. 1200 Eglinton Avenue East Suite 200 Don Mills, Ontario M3C 3N1
Macmillan Publishing Company is part of the Maxwell Communication Group of Companies.
First published in Great Britain in 1991 by Andersen Press Ltd., London.
First American edition 1993.
Color separated by Photolitho AG, Offsetreproduktionen, Gossau, Zürich.
Printed in Italy by Grafiche, AZ, Verona.
10 9 8 7 6 5 4 3 2 1
Library of Congress Cataloging-in-Publication Data
Brown, Ken, (Ken James)
Nellie's knot / written and illustrated by Ken Brown.
p.   cm.
Summary: Having tied a knot in her trunk to remind herself of
something very special, a baby elephant can't remember what it is.
ISBN 0-02-714930-7
[1. Elephants—Fiction. 2. Jungle animals—Fiction. 3. Memory—Fiction.] I. Title.
[PZ7.B8157Ne 1993] [E]—dc20 92-27910

Nellie's Knot

written and illustrated by
KEN BROWN

Four Winds Press ❋ *New York*

Maxwell Macmillan Canada *Toronto* Maxwell Macmillan International *New York Oxford Singapore Sydney*

Nellie had tied a knot in her trunk to
remind herself of something very special.
But now she had forgotten what it was! She
tried and tried, but she just couldn't remember.
"I'm not going to untie this knot until I do
remember," thought Nellie.

But a knot in your trunk gives you all sorts
of problems.
"Keep up, Nellie. Keep in line!"
But Nellie couldn't keep in line.

"Don't forget to wash behind your ears, Nellie!"
But Nellie couldn't wash behind her ears.

"Eat your breakfast, Nellie!"
But Nellie couldn't eat her breakfast.

"Catch the bananas, Nellie!"
But Nellie couldn't catch the bananas.

"Blow up the balloons, Nellie!"
But Nellie couldn't blow up the balloons.

"Help us put the streamers up, Nellie!"
But Nellie couldn't. She got into a
terrible tangle. Poor Nellie, she couldn't
do anything right, and she still couldn't
remember why she had tied a knot in
her trunk.

"Come and stir the cake, Nellie, and don't
forget to wish!" But, although Nellie
couldn't stir the cake, she *could* wish.
"I wish . . . I wish . . . I wish I knew why
I tied a knot in my trunk!"
But still Nellie couldn't remember.

She went off by herself to have a good, long think.

Then . . . as she was wandering sadly
through the jungle, not noticing where
she was going, she stumbled into a
clearing. All the animals seemed to be
having a party.

"Come on, Nellie! Blow out the candle!"

Nellie took a deep breath and
blew as hard as she could.
She blew so hard that out
went the candle . . . and
Nellie's knot!
"HAPPY BIRTHDAY, NELLIE!"

Suddenly, Nellie knew why she had tied a
knot in her trunk — to remember her birthday!